MW00973915

To
Camila,
I Love You All Ways.
From

....

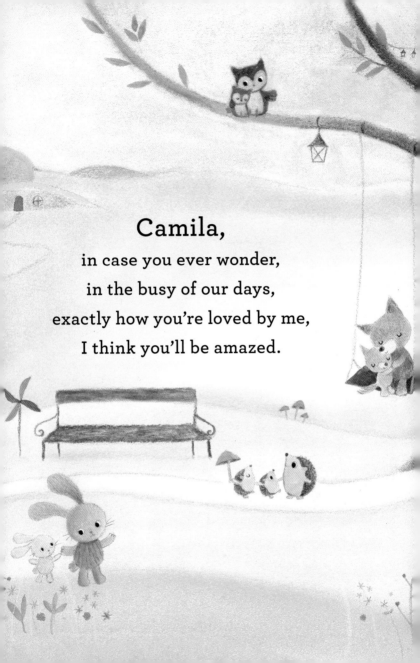

Camila,

in case you ever wonder,

in the busy of our days,

exactly how you're loved by me,

I think you'll be amazed.

Camila,

I love you first thing wide-awake

and nighttime sleepy too,

and every minute in between,
I love all the ways of you.

Camila,

I love you storytelling tales
to friends all gathered round

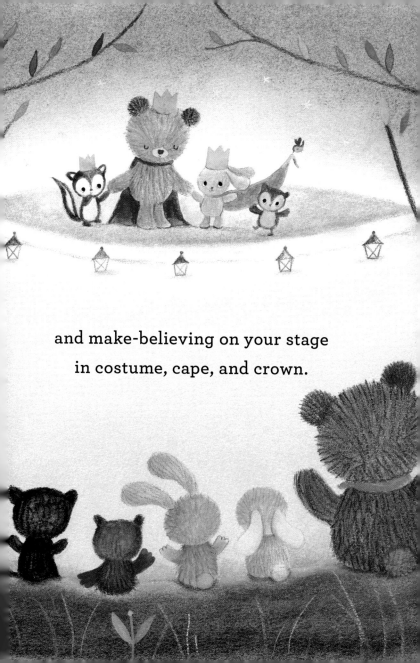

and make-believing on your stage
in costume, cape, and crown.

Camila,

I love you
underneath the sea

and side-by-side on land.

I love you
riding piggyback

and walking
hand-in-hand.

Camila,

I love you grumpy and upset,

excited, sassy, mad.

I love you cartwheel joyful

and under-blanket sad.

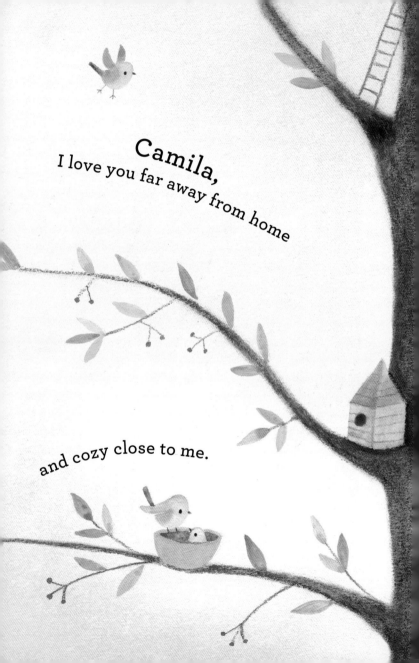

Camila,
I love you far away from home

and cozy close to me.

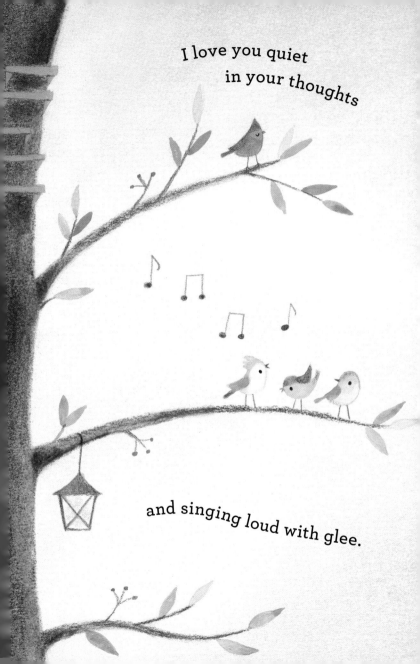

I love you quiet
in your thoughts

and singing loud with glee.

Camila,

I love you playing peekaboo
and swinging feet to sky.
I love you face up in the sun,
watching clouds go by.

Camila,

I love you covered

in the snow

and splashing

in the rain.

I love you mighty
mountain strong

and achy sick
with pain.

Camila,
I love you moody mischievous,
bending rules your way,

because my love is longer still
than any longest day.

Camila,

I love you at the age you are
and every year you grow

into more the special someone
I forever want to know.

Camila,

top to bottom, inside, through:

you're the certain of my days.

Camila,
no need to ever wonder more...
I love you all ways.

Camila,

draw a picture of your friends
and family that YOU love all ways!

Written by Marianne Richmond
Illustrated by Dubravka Kolanovic

Text copyright © 2020, 2023 by Marianne Richmond
Cover and internal illustrations © 2020, 2023 by Sourcebooks

This edition created by Bidu Bidu Books Ltd 2023

Put Me In The Story is a
registered trademark of Sourcebooks.
All rights reserved.

Published by Put Me In The Story,
a publication of Sourcebooks.
P.O. Box 4410, Naperville, Illinois 60567-4410
(630) 536-1104
putmeinthestory.com

Date of Production: September 2022
Run Number: 5026919
Printed and bound in China (GD)
10 9 8 7 6 5 4 3 2 1

MIX
Paper from
responsible sources
FSC® C117745
FSC
www.fsc.org

Bestselling books starring your child!
putmeinthestory.com